JOKER'S
Handbook

P9-API-797

Written by Ruth Thomson & Anne Civardi

Illustrated by Mark Oliver

Designed by Mei Lim

With special thanks to Lara

Contents

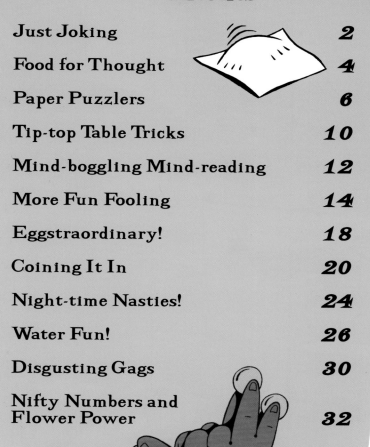

Just Joking

This Joker's Handbook is full of secrets on how to perform all kinds of tricks and jokes. There are some quick, easy tricks, some much trickier ones which need a little preparation and a few which are more difficult for which you may need an adult's help.

When you see this sign, it means you need a helper for the trick. Remember, a good trick is one that is safe and does not upset anyone. The tricks marked with a surprised face are a bit mischievous. It is best to play these on your friends and family. They are more likely to see the funny side and have a good laugh.

When you see an exclamation sign like the one pictured below, it means that you need to ask an adult to help you prepare the trick or joke.

Here are a few important tips and hints that all jokers should learn:

- Practice the trick in private so that you get it absolutely right. There is nothing worse than a trick that does not work.

- Always keep a straight face.

- Make up a few fun words to say as you perform the trick.

- Never do the same trick twice in front of the same people.

- Do not play too many tricks on the same person.

- Keep your best tricks up your sleeve for just the right moment.

*F*ood for Thought

All these fantastic tricks have something to do with food. Two of them need a little preparation, but it is worth the effort just to see the look on your victim's face.

Have a candy

The set up

For this trick, you need a shiny candy wrapper. Fold the wrapper in half and put your index finger inside it. Twist one end of the paper.

The trick

Cover the unwrapped part of your index finger with your thumb and bend your other fingers. Offer the 'candy' to a greedy friend and give him . . . a big surprise!

Brute strength

Challenge your friends to puncture a hole in a potato using only a paper drinking straw. When they have ended up with a pile of crumpled straws, show them the trick. Hold one finger over the end of the straw and stab the potato with as much force as you can. It works every time.

Thirsty work

The set up

Put a glass of juice under a cardboard box. Tell your audience that you will now drink the juice without touching the box.

The trick

Put your mouth close to the top of the box and mime drinking up the juice with loud slurping noises. Then announce that you have drunk the juice. One of the audience will not be able to resist lifting up the box. Quick as a flash, pick up the glass and drink the juice. Then you *really* will have done what you said you would.

Doing the splits

The set up

Choose a banana with a few black marks on it. Thread a sewing needle with a long length of thread. Leaving 2 inches of thread hanging outside, push the needle into the banana and out again a little further around it.

Push the needle back into the same hole and out again further around. Continue all around the banana back to the first hole. Each time, leave a little loop of thread. Pull both ends of the thread out of the banana and you will slice it inside. Do the same thing at intervals down the length of the banana.

The trick

Put the banana back in the fruit bowl. Wait for someone to unpeel it and just watch your victim's face!

5

*P*aper P*u*zzlers

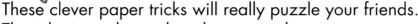

These clever paper tricks will really puzzle your friends. The joke is on them when they try to discover your tricky secrets!

Loopy paper

The set up

Cut a long strip of newspaper. Twist over one end and tape the ends together. Bet your friends that they cannot cut the loop in half and make it twice as long at the same time.

The trick

When your victim gives up, very carefully cut lengthwise down the center of the strip. Hey presto, your loop is twice as long.

Creepy crawler

The set up

Push a large strong rubber band through an empty cotton spool. Keep it in place with a small stick at one end (a). Make a hole in the middle of a small piece of candle. Push the free end of the band through it. Hold the band in place with a longer stick (b).

The trick

Wind the long stick around about 15 times. Put the cotton spool on the table while nobody is watching and cover it with a napkin. Watch your friends' faces as the napkin creeps across the table.

Postcard puzzle

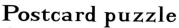

The set up
Challenge a friend to climb through a postcard.

The trick
Draw two spiral lines, one solid and one dotted. Cut along the solid line to the middle. Push the scissors into the middle of the card and cut along the dotted line. Now pull the card open!

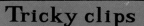

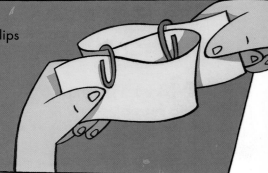

Tricky clips
Bet a friend you can link two paper clips together without even touching them. Fold a strip of paper, about 2 inches wide and 18 inches long, into an S shape. Attach two paper clips, as shown. Take an end of the paper in each hand and tug sharply.

Paper screecher!
Hold a small piece of paper between the first finger and thumb of both hands. Stretch it as tightly as possible, without ripping it. Put it up to your lips, but not inside your mouth, and blow hard. This makes a high screeching sound. The tighter you stretch the paper, the higher the screech will be.

A loud letter

The set up
Bend a paper clip into this shape and hook a rubber band across the ends. Fold a strip of card into three. Then tape one side of the paper clip to the middle fold. Put a small square of cardboard through the band.

The trick
Wind the cardboard square around until the band is very tight. Quickly fold the two flaps of card over it to stop the square from unwinding. Put the flapper into an envelope and give it to your friend. Just watch his face when he opens it.

Moving money

The set up
Tape a long, dark length of thread to the underneath of a $1 bill. Leave the bill lying around. Keep hold of the end of the thread and stay out of sight.

The trick
Someone is bound to stop and pick it up. Just as she stoops down to retrieve the note, whisk it away from under her nose! Meany!

A bag of candy

Bet you cannot fit more than one candy into an empty bag.

You cannot! After you put in one candy, the bag is no longer empty!

A bag of nothing

The set up

All you need for this trick is a small paper bag. Hold the bag in one hand, like this, with your index and fourth finger clasping it and your little finger, middle finger and thumb outside the bag.

The trick

With your other hand, pretend to throw something in the air which you then catch in the empty bag. Stare hard at the imaginary object as you throw. When you catch it in the bag, flick your thumb and middle finger against the side to make a realistic sound.

Tip-top Table Tricks

Here are some tricks to play at meal times. These will impress your friends and annoy your parents!

Spooning about

The set up

Challenge everyone at the table to balance a spoon on their noses.

The trick

While they are all busy dropping spoons, secretly lick your finger, wet the bowl of the spoon and quickly blow it dry. Now try putting it on your nose. Time how long it will stay there. Try to beat your record the next time you try this.

The musical wire

The set up

Fill two identical glasses a quarter full of water. Wet your forefinger and run it around the rim of each glass. If they make different sounds, add a little more water to one of the glasses until they are both in tune and sounding similar.

Now lay a thin, light wire or bobby pin, with the ends bent, over one glass and announce that you can make it dance without even touching it.

The trick

Rub the rim of the other glass with a wet finger. The glass with the wire will start to vibrate so that the wire or bobby pin dances!

A balancing act

The set up

Lay out three glasses and a piece of writing paper. Challenge someone to make a paper bridge between two of the glasses on which she can balance the third one.

The trick

Bend the paper in thin concertina folds across its whole width and lay it on top of two glasses. The third glass will then balance happily on the middle of it.

Nifty napkin

The set up

Spread a napkin flat on the table. Put a coin in the center of it. Ask people if they can pick up the napkin and turn it upright, without the coin falling out.

The trick

Hold two diagonally opposite corners of the napkin between each finger and thumb (with your thumb on top) and pull strongly. The napkin should fold in the middle, so that when you lift it up, the coin does not fall out.

Odd or even

The set up

In front of your audience, write the numbers 1-9 on a postcard, like this, and then tear the postcard into nine pieces. Drop them into a hat. Ask someone to blindfold you. Pick out one of the pieces and announce that you can tell whether you have picked an odd or even number.

The trick

Feel the edges of the piece you choose, before you lift it out. Even numbers all have *one* straight edge, whereas odd numbers have *two* straight edges apart from number 5 which has *none*.

Tell-tale fist

The set up

Tell your friends that you can guess which of them has a coin in their fist. Ask one of them to hold a coin tightly in a fist against his or her forehead, while you go out of the room. Slowly count to twenty. Come back in and ask everybody to hold out both their fists.

The trick

Quickly look at everyone's fists, while pretending to think deeply. The person with one fist paler than the other will be the one with the coin.

More Fun Fooling

Here are some tricks that your family and good friends might find pretty funny and pretty clever too. Be aware that these tricks could get you into deep trouble so it is best to choose people with a great sense of humor. Try not to catch them on a bad day.

Chalky chair

Put a stick of chalk between two pieces of paper and pound it into powder with something heavy. When your friend is not looking, sprinkle a little powder on her chair. You can guess what happens!

Tear it Up!

The set up

Make two tears in a piece of paper, as shown. Now challenge someone to tear it into three pieces holding it with both hands. It is impossible!

The trick

Hold the middle section in your mouth while you tear the paper apart.

A rude balloon

The set up

For this rather rude joke, you willl need a big, strong balloon and a flat ice-cream stick.

The trick

Put the stick into the neck of the balloon without puncturing it. Blow up the balloon a little. Make sure the neck is tightly stretched to stop the air from escaping. Put the balloon under the cushion of a chair. When your victim sits down, she might get a little red in the face!

Giant sneeze

Put a small bouncy rubber ball in the middle of a big handkerchief. Fix it in place with a rubber band. Pretend to sneeze so loudly into your hanky that it hurls it on to the floor. Watch your friends' faces when it bounces right back!

Orange teeth

Cut a quarter segment of orange peel from a big orange. Cut it, as shown, to make false teeth.

When someone asks you a question, pop the orange teeth into your mouth with the pith facing outwards. Now answer the question.

Nasty nosebleed

The set up

For this trick, you will need a helper and some fake blood.

The trick

Secretly pour some fake blood on a scrunched-up tissue. Ask your helper to tell your mom or dad that you have got a nasty nosebleed. Keep the pretense going for a couple of minutes before you come clean.

FAKE BLOOD RECIPE

4 teaspoons maple syrup
4 teaspoons water
Red and brown food coloring

Pour the maple syrup and water into a pan and ask an adult to help you heat it up. Stir the mixture. Then take it off the heat and let it cool. Add two drops of red food coloring and one drop of brown coloring. Keep your fake blood safe in a small bottle.

Ow!

The set up

Make a big bruise on your knee with some purple, black, yellow and red face paints. Use a small damp sponge to blend them smoothly together. It is best to practice using the face paints several times to get a really genuine-looking bruise.

The trick

Pretend to trip over when you walk into a room. Moan a bit while you are on the floor. When someone picks you up, hop about on one leg and show him your bruise.

What a bruiser!

Give yourself a black eye, again by blending purple, black, yellow and red face paints together. Then make up a real whopper about how you got it to tell your parents and friends.

Eggstraordinary

Eggs are good props for jokers. You can
make egg sandwiches when you have done the tricks!
Ask an adult to help you hard-boil half of them.

Raw or hard-boiled?

Take one raw and one hard-boiled
egg. Announce that you can tell which
one is hard-boiled without cracking either.
Spin both eggs on a smooth surface and then
lightly touch them. The hard-boiled egg will
stop immediately. The raw egg will move again
as soon as you lift your finger. Can you think why?

Spin both eggs again but, this time,
say you will tell which is which without
even touching them. The hard-boiled
egg will be the one that spins
longer and faster.

Now show you can spin the hard-
boiled egg for as long as you like.
Spin it on a small wooden tray.

If you gently turn the tray in the
opposite direction from that of
the spinning egg, the egg will
keep moving.

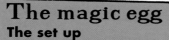

The magic egg

The set up

Pour water into two glasses. Add four tablespoons of salt to one glass and stir the water until all the salt has dissolved.

The trick

Innocently hand your victims the unsalted glass of water and challenge them to float one of the eggs in it. Whatever they do, the egg will sink! Now take your egg and put it into the glass of *salty* water. Your friends will be most surprised to see it float.

Stand to attention

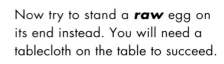

Make a **hard-boiled** egg stand on its end. One way to do this is to spin the egg very fast. As it spins, it will raise itself until it balances on one end.

Another way is to crush the shell at the larger end and rest the egg on the flattened shell.

Now try to stand a **raw** egg on its end instead. You will need a tablecloth on the table to succeed.

Wet the end of the egg and then dip it into some salt. Put the egg on the tablecloth, giving it a couple of twists before you carefully let go.

Once you have perfected all these tricks, challenge your friends to try.

Coining It In

Use your pocket money for these tricks or ask your victims to lend you a few coins. If you impress them enough, perhaps they will let you keep them!

A pushover

All you need for this trick are three coins.

The set up

Lay the coins in a row. Ask friends to move the coin on the left in-between the other two coins without either *moving* the middle coin or *touching* the right-hand one. (Saying these exact words are crucial to the success of this trick.)

The trick

Press a forefinger firmly on the middle coin. Slide the left-hand coin back with your free hand. Shove it sharply against the middle coin.

This will force the right-hand coin away, so that you can move the left-hand coin into the gap.

Tight-fisted

The set up

Ask someone to put his hands together like this, with the knuckles of the first and middle fingers and the tips of the ring and little fingers touching. Slide a coin between both pairs of fingers.

The trick

Now ask your victim to drop the coins while keeping the knuckles firmly together. It is impossible!

Scritch scratch

Do this trick on a table with a tablecloth.

The set up

Line up two big coins and a smaller one on a tablecloth. Turn a glass upside down and rest it on the two bigger coins. Challenge your friends to remove the trapped coin without touching either the other coins or the glass.

The trick

When everyone gives up, scratch the cloth in front of the glass pulling it towards you. The coin will slowly slide out.

Tricky coins

Put three coins in a row. Challenge friends to get rid of the middle coin without touching it. While they are still puzzling it out, take away one of the side coins and there will be no middle coin!

The immovable coin

The set up

Put a coin on your open palm. Announce that you will give the coin to anyone who can brush it off with a soft hair brush.

The trick

Your coin is safe! However hard anyone tries, the hairs of the brush will just slip over the coin and it will stay exactly where it is.

Pick it up

Ask a friend to stand with her heels against a wall and her feet together. Bet her that she cannot pick up a coin one foot in front of her without moving her feet or bending her knees.

It is impossible. She will either bend her knees or fall over!

Magic spinner

The set up

Rest a large coin upright on a flat, shiny surface with your right forefinger. Rub this finger with your left forefinger and explain that you are doing some magic.

Now rub your finger as far as the fingernail. Lift up both hands and the coin will spin away, as if by magic.

The trick

When you do the last rub of your finger, whizz your hand away and just catch the coin with the end of your thumb. This needs quite a lot of practice, but is very effective!

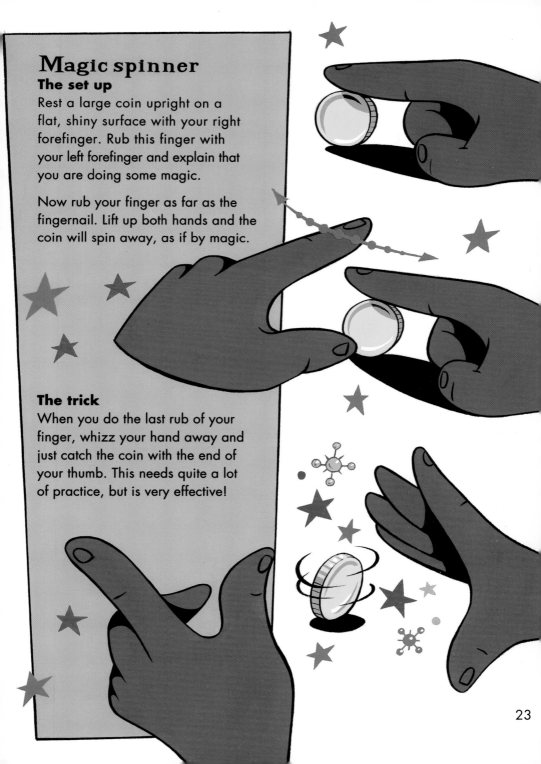

Mind-boggling Mind-reading

Amaze your family and friends with your superb mind-reading powers.

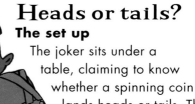

Heads or tails?

The set up

The joker sits under a table, claiming to know whether a spinning coin lands heads or tails. The helper and everybody else takes turns at spinning the coin.

The trick

If the coin lands 'heads,' the helper raises his right foot very slightly. If the coin lands 'tails,' the helper raises his left foot instead. The joker then has no trouble fooling everyone.

What's your name?

The set up

Tear some paper into slips. Ask everyone in turn to say a name. Pretend to write each name on a different slip. Fold up the slips and put them in a box. Ask someone to take out one slip and look at it. Then astound everyone by telling them the name on it.

The trick

Write down the first name you are given on *every* slip, so that you know the answer regardless of which slip is picked.

Night-time Nasties

Save these tricks for the night, when it is dark and your victims are ready for bed. To get the best results, you will have to prepare the tricks well in advance.

Popping peas

The set up

Tape together two plastic cups or empty yoghurt cups end to end. Stand them on a baking tray. Fill the top cup with dried peas.

The trick

Hide the tray and peas in your victim's room. Pour hot water into the cup with the peas. As they expand, the peas will plop out of the cup and on to the tray. This makes a very eerie pinging noise.

Terrifying tape

Record a nightmare tape to really terrify your victim. The secret is to leave some parts of the tape blank so that there are some quiet moments with no noises at all. Leave three minutes of the tape blank at the beginning, so that you have time to switch it on and leave the room before the sounds begin. Here are some really creepy, scary ideas: make a low pitched moaning sound; scratch your fingers against some fabric; hoot like an owl; drum your fingers on a hard surface.

Apple-pie bed

This is a joke that never fails to fool people. Make your victim's bed by folding the bed sheet in half and bringing the bottom edge over the comforter or blanket. Your victim will have a very tough time getting into bed!

Bed bugs

Put a small piece of fake fur inside the bottom of your victim's bed or, to be really nasty, you could put in an old banana skin.

Tee-hee!

Turning time forward

Before you go to bed, secretly turn all the clocks and watches in the house forward an hour, except for your own, of course. Get up as normal the next morning, then rush into your parents' room and tell them they have overslept!

Alarm bells!

If you want to be really mean, set your mom or dad's alarm clock for the middle of the night.

Water Fun!

Here are some really good water tricks to play on unsuspecting friends. Act as if nothing is going to happen to them and just watch their faces! Perform the messy tricks outside where it is easy to clear up afterwards.

Squirty drink

The set up

Make tiny pin holes near the bottom of an empty plastic bottle. Fill the bottle with water and screw on the lid as quickly and tightly as possible.

The trick

Hold the bottle upright and offer it to a friend to drink. When your victim unscrews the lid, the water will shoot out of the holes and soak him.

Water puzzle

Bet you cannot add something to a bucket of water to make it lighter.

Yes you can. Just make some holes in the bottom. The water will run out and the bucket will get lighter!

Help!

The set up

Half-fill a plastic cup with water. Stand on a chair and hold the cup against the ceiling. Keep it in place with a long stick or the handle of a broom and carefully get off the chair.

The trick

Ask a friend to hold the stick for you and tell him you are just going to fetch something else for the trick. When your victim takes hold of the stick, say 'Goodbye, see you later,' and run off with the chair.

String-along splash

The set up

Challenge a friend to pour water into a bowl that is over a yard away. For this, you will need a jug, a bowl, a piece of string, just more than a yard long, a teaspoon and water.

The trick

Put the spoon in the bowl. Tie one end of the string to the teaspoon and the other to the jug handle. Now fill the jug with water. Make sure the string goes across the spout and is as tight as possible, raise the jug and very carefully pour the water down the string and into the bowl.

Water challenge

The set up

Fill three glasses with water. Line them up with three empty glasses. Challenge a friend to change this line of glasses so that no full glass is next to another full one and no empty glass is next to an empty one. He is allowed to move only one glass.

The trick

It is easy! Just pour the water out of the second glass into the fifth one!

Now you see it, now you don't!

The set up

Fill a glass with water and place a coin, any size you like, under the glass. Ask your victim to look through the water at the coin and tell you that he can see it there. Now tell him that you will make the coin disappear.

The trick

With a wave of your arms and a few tricky words, cover the glass with a small plate. Now ask your friend to look through the glass again. The coin will have disappeared!

I told you so
The set up

Hold a glass of water in one hand and stretch your arm out in front of you. Bet a friend that even if he holds your outstretched arm with both hands, you will still be able to take a drink.

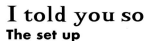

The trick

After struggling a little, take hold of the glass with your other hand and have a long, satisfying drink. You have won your bet!

What a corker!
The set up

Fill a glass with water to within 1 inch of the brim. Float a cork on the water and challenge a friend to make it float into the center without touching it. You will see that the cork stays against the side of the glass.

The trick

When your victim gives up, fill the glass so that the water is almost overflowing. Like magic, the cork will float into the middle.

29

Disgusting Gags

You will have to be a little careful about whom you play these tricks on. They will need to have a *really* good sense of humor. But after all, a joke is a joke!

What a sick joke!

The set up

Soften some ginger or chocolate chip cookies in some milk. When it is soft and slushy, it looks just like dog or cat barf.

Sneeze and spray

Dip your hand in water. Then sneak up on someone and fake a huge, out-of-control sneeze. At the same time, flick the water from your hand over your victim's head.

The trick

Leave the cookie mixture on the floor where someone is bound to spot it. When he does, he will probably say something like, 'Oh, yuk, look, the cat has been sick.' Go up to the 'barf', put your finger in it, lick your finger and say, 'Yup, it is sick alright.' Just watch the look on your victim's face!

Fake poo!

The set up

First turn the oven on to 350° F.

The trick

Mold a lump of salt dough into the shape of a dog's poo. Put it on a baking tray and bake it in the oven until it is hard – about 1 hour. Let it cool and then paint it brown. When it is dry, leave it where someone will spot it. You can also make disgusting salt dough cookies to give to unsuspecting victims.

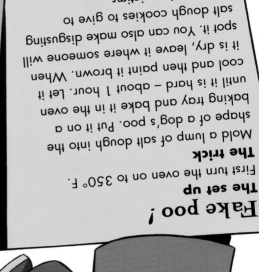

SALT DOUGH RECIPE

(This makes a big batch. If you store it in a plastic bag in the fridge, it will keep for a long time.)

Mix 10oz salt, 10oz plain flour and 1 tbs of oil together in a bowl. Mix in water, a little at a time, until you have a big ball of dough. Put the dough on a floured board and knead it with your hands until it is smooth and elastic. If it is too dry, add a little more water.

Tasty bogey

The set up

Squash a slice of ripe banana. Put it into the middle of a handkerchief.

The trick

In front of your victim, pretend to blow your nose hard. Make a big play of this. Then open up your hankie so he can see what is inside and eat the squashed banana. Yuk!

Nifty Numbers

The set up

Press out the eight cards in the pocket of the pack. Lay them in two rows in this order. You will see that the numbers in the top row add up to 19 and those in the bottom row add up to 20. Ask a friend to switch one card in the top row with one in the bottom row to make both rows add up to the same number. Is it possible?

The trick

Switch the 8 with the 9 and, at the same time, turn the 9 upside down to change it into a 6. Now both rows will add up to 18. Very nifty!

Flower Power

The set up

Press out the three Flower Power shapes in the pocket of the pack. Give them to a friend and challenge him or her to link them together as shown in this picture.

The trick

Fold the large rectangle in half, trying not to crease it (a). Slip the small square over the bottom prong of the folded rectangle (b). Fold the flower stem in half and hang it over the front edge of the same prong (c). Slide the small square over the flower stem and the end of the prong. Finally open out the large rectangle and, hey presto, you have linked the shapes together.